LIVING LEGALLY: SHORT STORIES BASED UPON THE INDIAN COURT SYSTEM

SIVA PRASAD BOSE

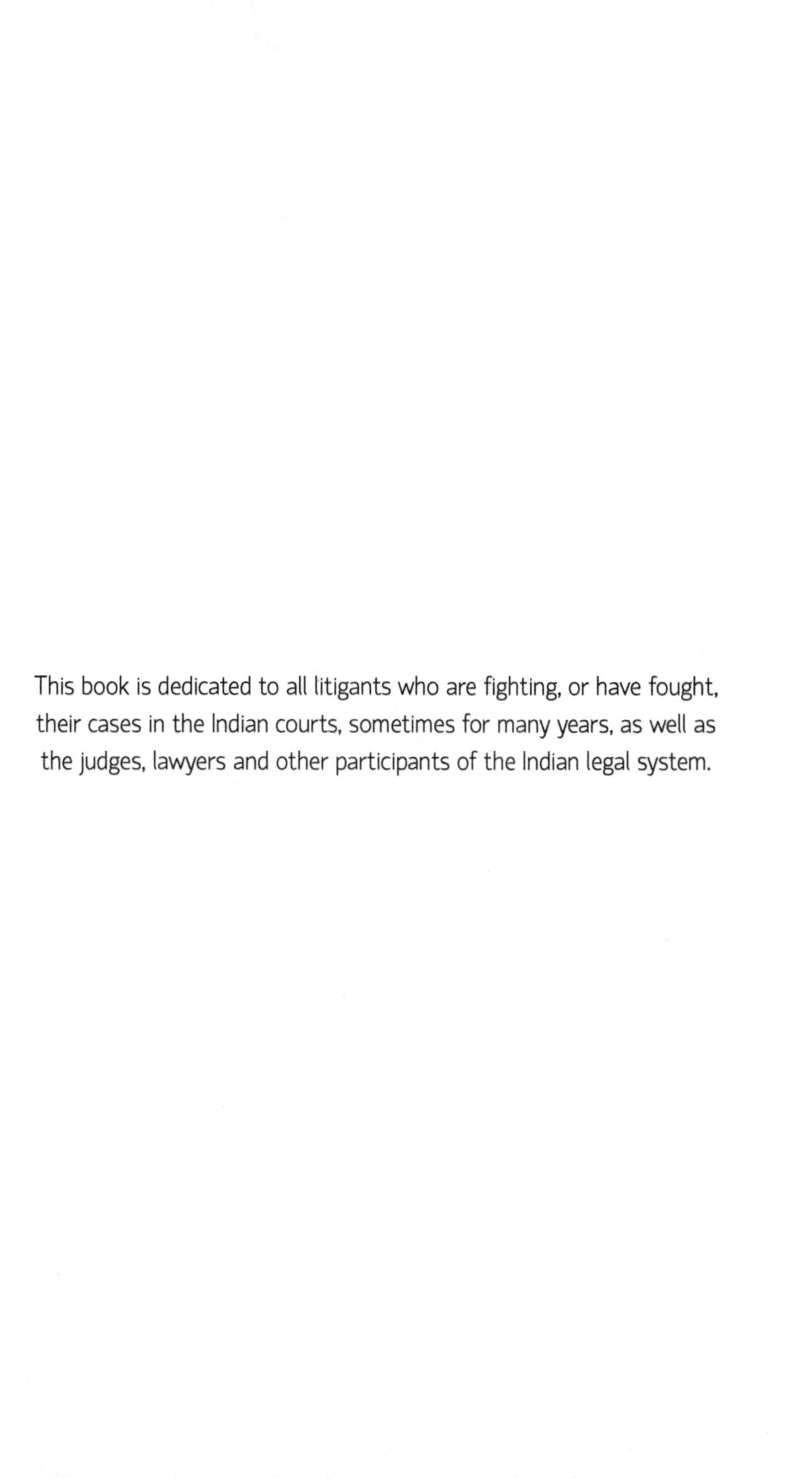

This book is dedicated to all litigants who are fighting, or have fought, their cases in the Indian courts, sometimes for many years, as well as the judges, lawyers and other participants of the Indian legal system.

Contents

Preface

The Indian court system is a large institution. There are thousands of cases being heard daily in the different courts of the land, big and small. Some of the cases run into years and others into decades. It thus affects lakhs or crores of people.

In this book, we write a few stories illustrating different aspects of the Indian court system, how it affects the common people in different situations of life. One of the stories is interpreting the timeless Indian epic, the Mahabharata, as a dispute fought in the Indian courts.

None of these stories are real, any similarity with persons living or dead is purely a matter of coincidence.

Our aim is to present the Indian court system from different viewpoints, and thus help the reader to gain an appreciation of the experience of different aspects of the court system for the common man. At the end of each story, we have added a section on lessons to learn from that story.

The intention is to show how the common man can succeed in getting justice if they persevere, even if the process is slow and fraught with difficulties.

Acknowledgements

The authors would like to pay their acknowledgements to many friends with whom they held conversations about the Indian court system as well as individual case situations.

We also would like to acknowledge the AI generated art by Midjourney AI, which was used for the illustrations in this book.

CHAPTER ONE

Mahabharata as a Court Case

Once there were two brothers named Dhritarashtra and Pandu who lived in a suburb in Delhi called Hastinapur with their parents. Their parents ran a comfortable business and their company was growing and profitable. They also had considerable property and assets.

Dhritarashtra was older than his brother Pandu by a couple of years. However, Dhritarashtra was partly disabled since he was blind from childhood. Therefore, he envied Pandu who was the favorite of their parents. Other than that, both the brothers did not have many problems. They lived in a comfortable upper middle-class home and shared everything they had. They lived as a joint family with aunts and uncles and other relatives in a big villa in a prime location.

When they grew up, both the brothers got married, Dhritarashtra to a girl named Gandhari and Pandu to a girl named Kunti. They soon gave birth to sons, Gandhari to a son named Duryodhana and Kunti to a son named Yudhisthira. Soon after the birth of Yudhisthira, Pandu got diagnosed with cancer and died prematurely. As a result, Dhritarashtra got to manage the family business as the CEO of the company after the death of their parents, with help from the other members of the extended family.

While growing up, at first the cousin brothers Yudhisthira and Duryodhana were friendly to each other and played and studied together and shared all their belongings. But as they grew up, jealousy developed inside Duryodhana towards his cousin brother Yudhisthira. Yudhisthira did well at studies in school while Duryodhana just managed to pass his exams. The same thing happened after school: Yudhisthira got admission in a top-ranking college and a decent job with a multinational corporation (MNC) after graduation. He also married a beautiful girl called Draupadi. Duryodhana just managed to get into a mediocre college and had to struggle for a few years before managing a low paying job. Moreover, his wife Bhanumati was not as good looking and skilled as Yudhisthira's wife Draupadi. Due to all these reasons, Duryodhana developed a lot of negative emotions towards his cousin brother.

After both Yudhisthira and Duryodhana had finished college and got some years of work experience, the time came for the family business to be split between them. Dhritarashtra was currently managing the company as CEO and was naturally partial to his own son Duryodhana. But on the advice of other elders in their joint family, he decided to split the shares 50:50 and hand roughly equal number of divisions of the company to each one.

This arrangement went on for a couple of years, each side managing their part of the business. Through capable strategic leadership and hard work, Yudhisthira was able to efficiently manage and grow his part of the company, while Duryodhana turned out a failure at managing his part of the business. This served only to further increase the jealousy Duryodhana felt towards Yudhisthira.

Aside from the jealousy of not doing as well as Yudhishthira, splitting the company 50:50 in the first place was not acceptable to Duryodhana who used to envy Yudhisthira and wanted full control of the company for himself. He felt that was his right in lieu of his father Dhritarashtra being the CEO of the business. So, with the help of his maternal uncle, Shakuni, he hatched upon a cunning plan.

Despite being blessed with many virtues and skills, Yudhisthira had one bad habit, in that he liked to gamble. Taking advantage of his weakness, Duryodhana and Shakuni challenged him to a game of dice whose terms were codified in a contract signed by both parties in the presence of witnesses.

As per the terms, if either party lost in the game of dice, he and his wife would have to go abroad for 12 years, and their business assets would be managed by the other party in their absence. On returning to India after 12 years, they would get back their share of 50% of the company and things would go back to the way they were earlier.

Yudhisthira fell for the bait and got defeated by Shakuni, who was the regional champion at gambling. Consequently, he had to go abroad as agreed and the 50% of the company was taken away by Duryodhana. As per the contract, Yudhishthira and his wife left India for 12 years and spent a few years in Europe as the export sales manager for the MNC where he was working.

Yudhishthira skillfully utilized his time abroad for upgrading his business skills and making new contacts through networking, while Duryodhana tried to cement his hold on the company with the help of a coterie of close advisors.

*Figure: Two persons playing a game of dice in India. AI
generated art by Midjourney AI*

After 12 years were over, Yudhisthira and his wife
Draupadi sought to return to India, and Yudhisthira sent
his wise friend and cousin Krishna to negotiate with
Duryodhana for getting back 50% of the company. When
Krishna arrived in Hastinapur to discuss terms,
Duryodhana flatly refused to share any part of the business
with his cousin brother as per the original contract. The
elders of the joint family also tried to reason with
Duryodhana, but to no avail.

Having no other option, Yudhisthira decided to file a court case against Duryodhana for getting control of his rightful part of the company, as per the original terms of the contract. The case was filed in Kurukshetra district court. Duryodhana, who was managing the business while Yudhisthira was abroad, by now had carefully cultivated an army of lawyers to fight the case on his behalf, while Yudhisthira mainly had his friend Krishna as his advisor.

Soon the court hearings started. Duryodhana's lawyers tried to make their case on the basis of forged documents showing that the company ownership was supposed to be his and the contract was void, while Yudhishthira's lawyers pleaded the court for enforcement of the original contract. Both the sides presented evidence and witnesses to support their case, however while Yudhishthira's witnesses and documents were genuine, those of Duryodhana's were forged and the witnesses coerced.

Figure: Scene in an Indian court. AI generated art by Midjourney AI

The Indian court system typically moves slowly. The process of presenting of arguments and hearings took a number of years. Since Yudhishthira's case had a stronger legal foundation, his case was stronger even though Duryodhana had hired many expensive lawyers. Eventually Yudhisthira won the case in the lower court, which ruled that the original contract was valid. But promptly Duryodhana appealed the verdict in higher courts. The case thus went on for 18 years, with each time Duryodhana losing and his lawyers appealing to a higher court. Duryodhana had to change his lawyers several times, since they kept losing in their arguments before the honorable judges.

While the case was going on, in the meantime Duryodhana also tried a few dirty tricks to intimidate Yudhishthira's side. These included tactics such as giving threats to Yudhishthira's family, defamatory articles posted in the local media with the help of paid journalists, creating obstructions for the electricity and water supply of the house where Yudhishthira was staying by bribing some municipal employees, and so on.

Many a times, because of all these tactics, Yudhisthira felt like giving up the court case and settling it, but his wise friend Krishna advised him to fight in search of justice without getting greedy or being attached to the eventual outcome of the court case. Because of this wise advice, Yudhishthira got the strength to fight on.

*Figure: Cross examination of witnesses in an Indian court.
AI generated art by Midjourney AI*

Eventually the appeals for the case reached the Supreme
Court of India. Yudhishthira's lawyers were able to
conclusively establish that Duryodhana's documents were
forged, and their contract was legally enforceable. As a
result, here too Duryodhana lost the appeal.

For all the years the court case was going on,
Yudhishthira managed his own career well and kept
working for the multinational company, where he kept
getting salary increments and promotions due to his hard

work. On the other hand, Duryodhana in his greed for control of the company made the mistake of focusing entirely on the court case and consequently was not able to increase his income or assets. His management of the company was also going poorly.

Consequently, once Duryodhana lost the court case, he had lost everything: he had few assets and his career was in shambles. In contrast, Yudhishthira now had a good position and a good job as well as winning the case. Thinking about this made Duryodhana mad with frustration. His mental health took a toll.

In his desperation, a few days later Duryodhana and a couple of acolytes crept into the premises of the company during the night and set fire to it. A lot of the assets of the company were damaged as a result. Yudhishthira lodged a police complaint and eventually Duryodhana was caught and jailed by the police.

Yudhishthira had managed to win the case after a long period of 18 years, but the company was in shambles due to mismanagement by Duryodhana and its assets burnt down. With great hard work and business skills gained over the years, Yudhishthira managed to rebuild the company back to prosperity and growth as its new CEO. The company went back to profitability and Yudhishthira was able to expand the business in various sectors and even overseas.

*Figure: Yudhishthira presiding over a board meeting of the
company as CEO. AI generated art by Midjourney AI*

Instead of enjoying a comfortable life as a co-owner
of the business, Duryodhana because of his jealousy and
deceit was financially ruined had now to spend his years in
jail.

Lesson from the story:

The Indian legal system can sometimes be slow in
delivering justice. Sometimes cases take years or even
decades in delivering a verdict, on top of it the execution
and appeals process can take even longer. To fight and win

such cases, one needs skills of perseverance, good time management, and a good plan. One also needs good friends one can turn to in times of trouble. It is important not to neglect one's own career when fighting the court cases. Also, one needs to pay attention to their physical and mental well-being. Being greedy for quick results and trying illegal actions does not pay in the long run, for the court system does manage to deliver justice to those who are hardworking and persistently fight their court cases against all odds.

CHAPTER TWO

Tale of the Stressed Judge

Vidyabhushan, one of the judges in a District Court, was a very busy man. He had a lot of cases pending before him. His superiors wanted him to close many of the cases by the end of the year, in order to improve their rate of disposal of cases. This was putting pressure on him.

Moreover, some of the cases involved politically influential people who were also starting to subtly put pressure on him to give a verdict in a certain way. There were constant media trials and social media scrutiny of court judgments. Vidyabhushan also had to manage his career to get timely promotions and keep up to date with the latest important judgements from the higher courts.

As a result of all this, Vidyabhushan had less time for personal life. Coming to court in the morning, sitting in the court all day, hearing arguments, giving judgments and hearing appeals were all physically exhausting for him.

Figure: Judge sitting in an Indian court. AI generated art by Midjourney AI

Often, Vidyabhushan had to take the case files home after work to read them before the next day's hearing. Also, he had to take care of his own family. When he went back home after a busy day at court, he had very less energy to tutor his daughter, who was giving her high school exams in a few months.

All the stress eventually took a toll on Vidyabhushan's health. He developed stress related sicknesses such as diabetes and had trouble sleeping and an erratic heartbeat.

He also began to be depressed sometimes. Soon, he had to miss case hearings multiple times due to ill health, which then affected his chances of promotion and led to further stress.

Eventually Vidyabhushan had to resign from his job in order to protect his mental and physical health from further damage. He then took a lighter job adjucating disputes which was less stressful than that of a full-time judge, but which also paid less.

Lesson from the story:

Judges in India have a high standing in society, yet their job too can be stressful. The huge caseloads and lack of sufficient new judge recruitments in the Indian legal system makes the life of existing judges more difficult. Litigants often do not appreciate the work involved and the mental stress of being a judge in Indian courts.

CHAPTER THREE

Tale of the Lazy Son and the Will

Once there was a rich farmer who owned some lands in a village in Karnataka state of India.

He had two sons. The elder son was industrious and hardworking while the younger one was lazy and greedy. To earn extra money and support his family, the elder son went to work in a city where he established a small business and was able to earn and save more money than if he had just stayed in the village. The younger son, being lazy, just stayed and helped to cultivate his father's lands, hoping secretly that his father will leave him all the lands after his death. However, the farmer father loved both sons equally and did not show any partiality towards any son.

After some years, the farmer died. Before dying, he wrote a will and divided his lands equally between the two sons. The elder son was quite happy with this, but the younger was not, since he wanted to occupy the whole land and felt that the fact he had stayed with his father entitled him to get the complete land. Therefore, he felt that it was his right to occupy the whole of it rather than give away half to his elder brother who lived in the city and only occasionally came to the village to visit.

Additionally, since he was living with his father and taking care of his fields, he already had the advantage of possession of the property and vowed never to give it up, regardless of what his father wished, or his elder brother would do.

To get the whole land, the younger son managed to forge a copy of the will by forging his father's signature. In the forged will, the entire land was given to him and none to the elder son. In this way, there were two versions of the farmers's will, in one version both the sons were getting an equal share and in the other all of it was going to one son and none to the other. Additionally, the younger son succeeded in registering his forged copy of the will with the local registry office in the tehsil by paying bribes to the local registrar.

When the elder son went to court to enforce the original will of his father, the younger one opposed it saying that his forged copy, that gave the entire land to him, was the real version. Soon the case ended up in court.

Figure: A busy court scene in India. AI generated art by Midjourney AI

Like in most lower court cases involving property disputes, the case dragged on for years. It was a painful task to go to the capital of the district to attend the court hearings. Many times, the hearings were adjourned and the judge was transferred and the new judge took additional time to hear the case.

The younger son also tried various cunning tactics such as filing new cases on petty pretexts, just to further delay the case and enjoy his possession of the father's land for longer while the case dragged on and on. He also bribed some local witnesses to give false testimonies of his father's wishes before he died, to build the case that his version of the will was true.

In this way the case went on for more than 10 years. The elder brother almost wanted to give up the case, considering how much effort he had to go through to hire a lawyer, pay the lawyers fees, travel to the district court on the court date and so on. Yet, for the interest of justice, he felt like fighting on. He was certainly earning more money from his business in the town than his brother was, even though his brother had the advantage of possession of the property and local witnesses whom he could bribe.

After many years, the case finally case to the final stage of evidence. Despite all kinds of tactics and threats by the younger son, the elder son's lawyer managed to get the court to agree on a forensic scan of the two wills from the government laboratory, to establish which will was genuine and which was forged. As a result, he was able to show that his younger brother's will was the forged one. He thus managed to win the case and justice was served. The court ruled that as per the genuine will, the father's land should be equally divided between his two sons.

Even after winning the case, the elder son's problems were not over. Since the younger son still had possession and refused to hand over the elder son's share of the land, he again had to apply for execution of the judgment, which took some more time but eventually succeeded. The younger son, to further delay the case, contemplated an appeal in the higher courts, but eventually gave up once he found out the cost of such an appeal. So, after all these years, the elder son finally got his just inheritance.

Lesson from the story:

Property disputes, concerning wills and property sharing, often within members of the same extended family, sometimes take many years or even decades to get justice in the courts. One should not let this unfortunate fact make them lose faith in justice. By fighting a resolute battle and not being scared or expecting quick justice, but by perseverance, justice will be delivered in the courts. Justice may be late sometimes but is never lost.

CHAPTER FOUR

Story of the Bad Neighbor

There was an old couple, Mr. and Mrs. Tripathi, who lived alone in a house in a big city. They had a son, but he was living with his family in a distant city and only occasionally came to visit them. Now, the house of Mr. Tripathi was located in a posh locality, and could fetch a very good price when sold. So, it caught the eye of a cunning neighbor named Mr. Balwant who was living in a nearby house in the same locality.

Figure: Old couple living in a house in India. AI generated art by Midjourney AI

Balwant thought, what if I could just make life so unbearable for the old couple, that they would be forced to sell or leave their house and then I could get it for free or for a very low price. Thus thinking, he developed a plan to harass and drive away the Tripathi couple. Balwant's scheming wife also helped him to refine the plan and make it fool-proof.

Soon after, Mr. and Mrs. Tripathi went to visit their son and daughter in law for a month. But on returning to their home after one month, the couple started having a number of daily problems. Their electricity bill became unbearably high, so did their water bill, the water got cut at random hours, their mailbox was broken and newspapers and mail in the mailbox started getting stolen, their daily domestic workers started getting threats, there was garbage on their front lawn and so on.

Unknown to the Tripathi couple, when they were gone the cunning neighbor Balwant had some wires installed to steal their electricity and employed a plumber to install extra pipes and taps to divert their municipal water supply and control it. He also started tactics such as threatening the domestic help of the old couple, breaking the mailbox and stealing stuff from it and leaving garbage about. Such incidents of harassment gradually increased month by month.

Eventually the Tripathis came to know who was responsible and went to Balwant's house to complain, but Balwant refused to stop and further threatened them instead. This led to an argument and Balwant pushed Mr. Tripathi, who fell to the ground and hurt himself.

Figure: Old man in an argument with a neighbor. AI generated art by Midjourney AI

Initially, Mr. Tripathi did not report the incidents to the police since he was afraid of the police and unfamiliar with their procedures, being old and frail. But as the harassment incidents from Balwant became more and more frequent, Mr. Tripathi was left with no option and had to approach the local police in the city to file a complaint.

But the police were, as is often the case in India, reluctant to register an FIR in order to avoid extra work and improve their statistics of lodged FIRs. They demanded proofs such as video evidence which Mr. Tripathi was unable to collect, being aged and unfamiliar with technology. As a result, the police took no concrete action but only promised the Tripathi couple to send a beat policeman once every other month to check on their safety.

Finally, the Tripathi couple became desperate and with the help of their son and some local friends, hired a lawyer to get the courts to come to their aid. The lawyer sent a legal notice to Balwant to stop the harassment actions, and also filed a case in the civil court to force the police to file an FIR and investigate the ongoing complaints. They also made a complaint with the SDM of the district under the Senior Citizens Protection Act.

Eventually, with the commencement of the legal case, the local police were forced to register a case. Soon, the police came to Mr. Balwant's house to interview him, with which Balwant got a little scared. The incidents of threats and other harassment by Balwant soon stopped. Mrs. Tripathi got a few people to fix their water and electricity supply. Balwant's plan to drive away the couple by harassing them and get their house cheaply thus got foiled.

Lesson from the story:

Sometimes, the senior citizens are seen as soft targets by unscrupulous people eyeing their property. The law has some safeguards for the protection of senior citizens from abuse and such safeguards can be utilized skillfully. It is important for senior citizens and their well wishers to keep abreast of existing laws and mechanisms for their protection and utilize them as needed.

CHAPTER FIVE

Tale of the Vengeful Wife

Once there was a man named Amit who was working as a software engineer in a company in a big city. Like most software engineers, he had to work long hours and was still always afraid of getting fired. However, his salary was decent even though he did not get too many increments or promotions. He even managed to save enough money for buying a small apartment, with the help of bank loans.

Eventually his parents pressurized him to get married. His wife Sunita was from a small town and was unfamiliar with IT lifestyle of long working hours and stressful jobs with no job security. Sunita's father was a police officer in their town. Soon after the marriage, Sunita moved to live in the city with her new husband Amit.

Figure: Indian wedding scene. AI generated art by
Midjourney AI

Initially their marriage was going well and both had a happy life. However, it soon became apparent there was a mismatch of expectations. The wife Sunita was expecting a life of comfort with the husband Amit's salary. She was not used to the pressures of living in a big city and having to deal with Amit's long working hours and the insecure nature of his IT job.

This mismatch of expectations led to domestic fights between Amit and Sunita only a few months into their marriage. The fights soon increased in intensity and frequency. The neighbors too got concerned about the brawls that were often in late hours after Amit returned from his office.

Figure: Argument between husband and wife in India. AI generated art by Midjourney AI

One day Amit and Sunita had a huge fight and Sunita left for her mother's place in a huff. There, she spoke to friends and found out about the wife friendly laws such as 498a (anti dowry act) and DV (prevention of domestic violence act) which did not need much proof aside of allegations, and which she could use to blackmail her husband for a huge amount of money.

Sunita also found a greedy lawyer who was all too happy to help her write the false allegations that are needed for 498a and DV, even though Amit's family had never really pressurized her for dowry. The lawyer only wanted 10% of the final settlement from the husband Amit after the case was won, which he was confident he would be able to get at least 1 crore as the settlement amount.

Sunita and her lawyer went to a mahila thana (women's police station) in their town and filed the complaint for 498a and domestic violence, naming the husband Amit and all his family members including Amit's old mother and father and even Amit's sister as accomplices.

Soon after, Amit received a call from the local police inspector informing him that an FIR had been lodged on behalf of his wife, and asking him to come to the police station to join the investigation.

Amit was pretty shocked on getting the call from the police, for he had no idea that his wife Sunita would go to this extent due to just some domestic fights. When he went to the police station, the police threatened to arrest him and openly asked for Rs 20000 as bribe to remove the names of his parents and sister from the FIR, and Amit felt he had no choice but to pay the same.

Figure: Cross examination scene in an Indian court. AI generated art by Midjourney AI

Soon the court dates started, which were in Sunita's hometown. To fight the case, Amit had to hire a local lawyer in his wife's hometown, take leaves from his work and attend each of the court dates. The local lawyer, however, turned out to be unreliable and more interested in milking Amit for his money than in actually fighting the case. All this caused a lot of stress to Amit and impacted his work performance, which led to him being fired from his job. With great difficulty he was able to find another, slightly lower paying, IT job in a different company.

Being desperate, Amit managed to find a group of people in his city who were trapped in similar kinds of cases and could support each other. With their help, he managed to get a more decent lawyer and formulate a strategy to fight the false cases.

Figure: Lawyer arguing a case in an Indian court. AI generated art by Midjourney AI

The 498 and DV cases dragged on for a few years. By now Amit had gotten experienced in how these things worked and how best to collect the evidence to disprove the false allegations of his wife Sunita. Eventually, the court found him not guilty.

Being left with no options, Sunita's side then came forward to compromise and they were able to jointly file for a Section 13B mutual consent divorce petition, which got approved in its due time. Finally, Amit was able to break free from the stress of the court cases and remarry.

But alas, all these years of running around the courts had stunted Amit's career growth and wages, and also had a toll on his father who had passed away in the midst of the case. Despite this, Amit had now found a new confidence to handle any and all court cases that might come his way and his determination, hard work and support from the well wishers had finally paid off.

Lesson from the story:

Some laws in India are easy to be misused by unscrupulous people, and this can cause a lot of suffering for the affected persons and their families. The way out is to be determined and persistent in the cause of justice and not to be swayed by threats of police etc.

If a person is persistent and ready to fight, despite all the drawbacks of the implementation of the laws, they will eventually win justice in the Indian courts.

Therefore, in the face of false cases and setbacks, one should never get depressed or distressed, but fight on with determination.

Tale of the Greedy Lawyer

Once there was a big and famous senior lawyer named Sudarshan who lived in a medium sized town in India. Even though it was not a big city, it had plenty of cases of all kinds: property disputes, criminal cases, family disputes, matrimonial cases and so on. As a result of hard work, Sudarshan became famous in the town and even all over the state. People came from far away to request him to take their case. He started charging unusually high fees and still the people were ready to pay whatever he asked.

Figure: Lawyer arguing a case in an Indian court. AI generated art by Midjourney AI

When he was a junior lawyer, Sudarshan used to be careful and ethical about which cases to take and which not to. He would not take on cases unless he was himself convinced of his client being in the right. However, as he became big and famous, Sudarshan stopped evaluating cases and took on any case where the client could afford his fees.

Once Sudarshan was approached by rich client regarding a new case. The client was a businessman and wanted his help in a fraud case. As was now his standard practice, Sudarshan took on the case without much analysis, simply because the client agreed to pay him a huge bonus on top of his regular fees.

Later, after a few hearings had passed, Sudarshan felt that the client's case was weak as per the law and the opposite party's case was strong. To keep his record unblemished, he wanted desperately to get off the case. Moreover, more than half of his fees had already been paid by the client by then.

All Sudarshan wanted was some plausible pretext to leave the case. With this in mind, Sudarshan started missing to appear on some of the case dates. Also, while the first case hearings were going on, the opposite party brought a perjury case on Sudarshan's client. Instead of fighting the new case as well, Sudarshan took the opportunity to tell the client that this new case was not agreed in advance, he had no time from the existing case load and therefore the client needed to hire a new lawyer for the same.

The client had no choice but to engage a new lawyer for the ongoing case as well as the new case. However, when he came to Sudarshan to collect his case documents, Sudarshan demanded an additional hefty sum of money failing which he would keep the client's case files and not give a no objection certificate.

The client was by then quite angry at Sudarshan's refusal to cooperate, his frequent absences and now his refusal to release his documents bants without taking an additional hefty amount. So, he complained to the bar council about Sudarshan's conduct and sought the help of the bar council to get Sudarshan to release his case documents.

The bar council, after a couple of hearings, then ordered Sudarshan to release the case files to the client. Sudarshan had no choice but to do the same. Moreover, his client, who was a moderately influential person in the town, spread the word around about Sudarshan's conduct regarding his case.

As a result, Sudarshan's clients slowly started to decrease. Soon, Sudarshan was struggling to get enough new clients who could afford his fees. He started to reflect what had gone wrong, from being the top lawyer in demand in the city and probably even the state to the place where he was now, with not enough clients hiring him. He realized that in his greed for money, he had unwittingly ended up sacrificing his professionalism, and this had hurt his promising career.

Lesson from the story:

While most of the lawyers may be honest and hardworking, sometimes one may get a lawyer who is unscrupulous and cares more about the client's money than about fighting the case.

In such cases, the clients should not be afraid to demand professional conduct from their lawyer and failing the same not be afraid to change their lawyer for a better one.

Clients in Indian court cases need to cultivate the skills to hire principled and hardworking lawyers, manage their lawyers properly and fight the case together.

CHAPTER SEVEN

Story of the First Day

"How dare they try to take my property from me!"

Thoughts raged in Ravi's mind. For today was the date his court case was going to start. The case he had been waiting for the last three years. The case which would bring back his self-esteem, finally redeeming it from years of humiliation, by his own siblings no less.

"What didn't I do for my brothers, and this is how they repay me!"

"Today I will show them all what a court case is really like!"

But Ravi also had a few thoughts full of doubt. "But what if my lawyer doesn't turn up, after charging me so much money? Or worse, what if he is allied to the opposite party and taken money from them?"

Raging with thoughts of anger, confusion, fear and a myriad of other emotions, Ravi called his lawyer. "Awasthi Sir, are you coming to the court? I am already driving there! We must not be late!"

The lawyer tried to calm him down "Don't worry Mr. Ravi, I am only stuck in a bit of traffic jam. Anyway, I have asked my subordinate to be there and he has almost reached the court premises." Eventually, the lawyer arrived, and Ravi reached the court with his lawyer but after a delay of 20 minutes.

After a security check and with some effort, Ravi and his lawyer located the right courtroom where their case hearing was fixed. Their hearing was listed at number 6 in the day's schedule. So, they went to the courtroom and waited. Their opposite party and their lawyer were also present.

However, 30 minutes had passed since the courtroom opened, it was full of people and only the judge was missing. Ravi waited and waited, with great anticipation and full of expectations as to what might happen.

*Figure: A busy court hearing in India. AI generated art by
Midjourney AI*

After 35 minutes, the clerk announced that the judge was on leave and therefore won't be coming that day. They announced the next hearing date which was 2 months away. On hearing this, Ravi got a huge shock. All his expectations were in the mud. He almost fainted, but then managed to compose himself.

Soon the days became months, months became years and the court hearings continued at a snail's pace. Ravi finally understood that he would have to be patient to get his much-anticipated revenge. Very, very patient.

Lesson from the story:

This story illustrates the futility of expecting a quick justice from the Indian courts. Even though some people may feel they are in the right, the court system can be sometimes slow and it can take years or even decades for justice to be delivered.

The qualities of hard work, thorough case building, effective time management and persistence are invaluable qualities for any litigant fighting cases in Indian courts.

About The Authors

Siva Prasad Bose is a writer of introductory guidebooks on different aspects of Indian laws. He is also a retired electrical engineer, retired after many years of service in Uttar Pradesh Power Corporation Limited. He received his engineering degree from Jadavpur University, Kolkata and has a law degree from Meerut University, Meerut and a Bachelor of Science from MMH University Ghaziabad. His interests lie in the fields of family law, civil law, law of contracts, and areas of law related to power electricity related issues.

Joy Bose is a researcher and data scientist.

Other Books By Siva Prasad Bose

- Introduction to Wills and Probate
- Delays in Court Cases in India
- Introduction to Negotiable Instruments
- Introduction to Marriage Laws in India
- Neighbor Problems in India and what to do about them
- Managing Court Cases with Mental Strength
- Introduction to Patents and Patent Law in India
- Introduction to Property Law in India

www.ingramcontent.com/pod-product-compliance
Lightning Source LLC
Chambersburg PA
CBHW022119150726
47990CB00003B/1422